PLANTING EQUIPMENT

Therese M. Shea

Enslow Publishing
101 W. 23rd Street
Suite 240
New York, NY 10011
USA
enslow.com

WORDS TO KNOW

accurate Not having mistakes; able to hit a point exactly.

acre A measure of land that equals 4,840 square yards (about 4,047 square meters).

compressed Pressed or squeezed together.

crop A plant that is grown by farmers.

distance The amount of space between two things.

equipment Tools needed for a job.

GPS Global Positioning System. A radio system that uses signals from satellites (machines in space) to tell you where you are and to give you directions to other places.

nitrogen A gas that helps plants stay healthy.

CONTENTS

Seeds can be planted by hand in a small garden.

How a Garden Grows

You probably know how plants grow. You plant seeds in soil in a sunny place and water them. Plants grow! Farms need to plant many seeds to grow many crops.

FAST FACT
Plant seeds grow roots and then grow up to break through the soil.

Farmers need special machines to help them plant lots of crops.

So Many Seeds

Some farms are very large. They may have hundreds of acres. Farmers plant many crops. They could plant the seeds by hand. But planting equipment makes the job easier and faster.

FAST FACT
Another word for planting seeds is "sowing."

A broadcast seeder is useful for spreading seeds over a large area.

Many Kinds

There are many kinds of seeds. They are planted in different ways. Some need to be deep under the ground. Some can be spread on top. There are many kinds of planters, too.

FAST FACT
A broadcast seeder spreads grass seeds on top of the soil.

Air seeders do many jobs at once. Farmers adjust them based on the crop.

Air Seeders

Farmers use air seeders to plant small, round seeds. These machines use compressed air to sow seeds. The machine puts fertilizer and nitrogen in the ground. This helps plants grow.

FAST FACT
Fertilizer is any matter added to soil to help plants grow.

The seed drill has different parts to drill into the soil and plant seeds.

Seed Drills

Many farms use seed drills to plant seeds. First, the machine drills into the earth. Then, it plants the seeds. Finally, the machine places soil over the seeds.

FAST FACT
Seed drills are used to sow smaller seeds, like wheat seeds.

The planter places the seeds in neat rows.

Planters

The planter is the most accurate planting machine. It makes sure seeds are planted with a certain distance between them. That way, plants have plenty of room to grow.

Fast Fact
Planters are used for larger seeds, like corn.

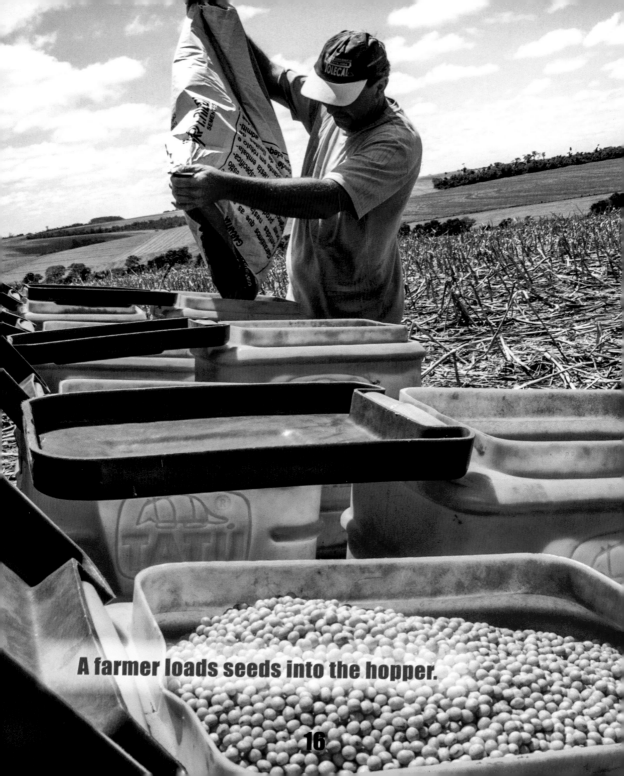

A farmer loads seeds into the hopper.

In the Hopper

Some planters have a box with seeds for each row. Others use one big seed box. Seeds travel from the seed box through tubes to each row. The seed boxes are sometimes called hoppers.

A farmer uses a computer in his tractor to help him plant seeds.

Surprising Machines

Some planters sow two kinds of crops at once. Some use computers to keep track of where and how much to plant. GPS can help planters sow a corn maze!

FAST FACT
Tractors pull most planters.

Today's huge planters allow farmers to plant many seeds at one time.

A Huge Help

One of the biggest planters in the world is 120 feet (37 meters) wide. It plants 48 rows of seeds at the same time. What an amazing farm machine!

Activity

Crop in a Straw

You can see how a seed grows into a plant—in a straw!

YOU WILL NEED:
- 2 wheat seeds
- 2 see-through drinking straws
- paper towel
- plastic cup
- water

Step 1: Twist a strip of paper towel until it's thin enough to stick into each straw about 3 inches (7.6 cm). A bit should stick out. You may need an adult to help.

Step 2: Place the wheat seeds into the other ends of the straws. They should rest on top of the paper towel.

Step 3: Place the straws into a plastic cup with a few inches of water in it. The paper towels will soak up the water.

Step 4: Watch your seeds for signs of growth!

LEARN MORE

Books

Dittmer, Lori. *Seeders*. Mankato, MN: Creative Education, 2018.

Dufek, Holly. *Planters & Cultivators with Casey & Friends*. Austin, TX: Octane Press, 2016.

Waldendorf, Kurt. *Hooray for Farmers!* Minneapolis, MN: Lerner, 2016.

Websites

How Do Seeds Sprout?
wonderopolis.org / wonder / how-do-seeds-sprout
Find out more about what happens to seeds under the ground.

Types of Seeders
farmingequipmentcanada.com / farming-equipment-canada / types-of-seeders /
Read more about each kind of planting equipment.

INDEX

Published in 2020 by Enslow Publishing, LLC.
101 W. 23rd Street, Suite 240, New York, NY 10011
Copyright © 2020 by Enslow Publishing, LLC.
All rights reserved.
No part of this book may be reproduced by any means without the written permission of the publisher.

Library of Congress Cataloging-in-Publication Data

Names: Shea, Therese M., author. |
Title: Planting equipment / Therese M. Shea.
Description: New York : Enslow Publishing, 2020. | Series: Let's learn about farm machines | Includes bibliographical references and index. | Audience: Grades K-3.
Identifiers: LCCN 2019006970| ISBN 9781978513150 (library bound) | ISBN 9781978513136 (pbk.) | ISBN 9781978513143 (6 pack)
Subjects: LCSH: Planters (Agricultural machinery)--Juvenile literature. |Planting (Plant culture)--Juvenile literature.
Classification: LCC TJ1483 .S543 2020 | DDC 631.5/310284--dc23
LC record available at https://lccn.loc.gov/2019006970

Printed in the United States of America

To Our Readers: We have done our best to make sure all website addresses in this book were active and appropriate when we went to press. However, the author and the publisher have no control over and assume no liability for the material available on those websites or on any websites they may link to. Any comments or suggestions can be sent by e-mail to customerservice@enslow.com.

Photos Credits: Cover, p. 1 Fotokostic/Shutterstock.com; interior pages background landscape Jurgis Mankauskas/Shutterstock.com; p. 4 Chepko Danil Vitalevich/Shutterstock.com; pp. 5, 7, 9, 11, 13, 15, 17, 19, 22 (hay bale) photomaster/Shutterstock.com; p. 6 naramit/Shutterstock.com; p. 8 Fotokostic/Shutterstock.com; p. 10 Vadim Orlov/Shutterstock.com; p. 12 Baloncici/Shutterstock.com; p. 14 bbernard/Shutterstock.com; p. 16 Alf Ribeiro/Shutterstock.com; p. 18 Bloomberg/Getty Images; p. 20 Design Pics Inc/Alamy Stock Photo; p. 23 © iStockphoto.com/ilyakalinin; cover, p. 1 logo element (tractor) Krivosheev Vitaly/Shutterstock.com